SPACESHIP NUMBER FOUR

A THANKSGIVING STORY

TO CARL
Thanks to Emma and Jacob

First Edition   1   2   3   4   5   6   7   8   9   10

Library of Congress Cataloging in Publication Data
Wunsch, Marjory.   Spaceship number four : a Thanksgiving story / story and pictures by Marjory Wunsch.
    p.   cm.   Summary: While at her grandparents' house for Thanksgiving dinner, Molly builds a wooden spaceship that takes the family cat on an outer space adventure.   ISBN 0-688-10472-X.—ISBN 0-688-10473-8 (lib. bdg.)   [1. Thanksgiving Day—Fiction.   2. Cats—Fiction.   3. Interplanetary voyages—Fiction.]   I. Title.   PZ7.W9643Sp   1992   [E]—dc20   91-27552   CIP   AC

SPACESHIP NUMBER FOUR
A THANKSGIVING STORY

STORY & PICTURES BY MARJORY WUNSCH

LOTHROP, LEE & SHEPARD BOOKS   NEW YORK

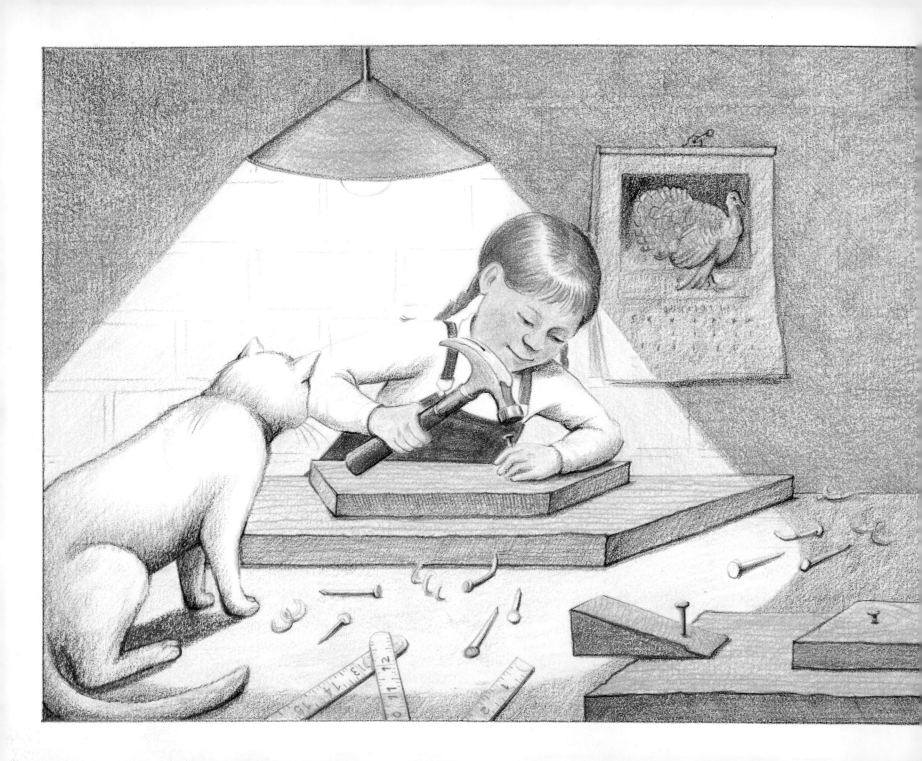

It was Thanksgiving Day. Down in Grandpa Harry's basement workshop, Molly finished her fourth, and finest, wooden spaceship. Mordecai looked on.

Molly showed SPACESHIP NUMBER FOUR to all the relatives who had gathered at Grandma and Grandpa's for the holiday.

"I know, don't tell me. It's the *Mayflower*!" said Great-Uncle Herman.

"She's so-o-o creative!" gushed Aunt Nicole.

"Buzz off, kid!" snapped Cousin Henry.

On the back porch, Molly loaded the ship and assembled her crew. "Ten, nine, eight…" She was approaching blastoff when Grandma Helen opened the back door.

"Dinner is ready," Grandma announced.

Everyone sat down to a grand Thanksgiving feast. Turkey and stuffing were delicious, but Molly was longing to play with SPACESHIP NUMBER FOUR. So, right after pumpkin pie, she mumbled, "Thankyouforeverythingmayipleasebeexcused," and ran off without waiting for an answer.

Molly headed straight for the back porch, but when she looked out the window, she saw no sign of her spaceship. That's odd, she thought. I wonder where it is.

She began her search for the missing craft in the living room. Cousin Harvey was on the rocking horse, heading west. "Have you seen my spaceship?" asked Molly. "Nope, only deer and antelope," yelled Harvey. Molly moved on.

She tried the garage next but found only Uncle Morris, arriving late as usual. "Have you seen a spaceship?" asked Molly.

"No," said Uncle Morris. "Just lots of cars heading for turkey dinners."

So Molly ran back to the dining room, where Grandma Helen was clearing the table. There were mounds of crumbs and mountains of dirty dishes. But still no spaceship.

In the den, Molly asked Uncle Bernie and Uncle Bill if *they* had seen a lost spaceship.

"Nothing here," mumbled the uncles, who looked a little lost themselves.

Molly walked to the guest room. There was Aunt Flo, saying good-bye to Aunt Sadie, who lived far away in Florida. There was no spaceship.

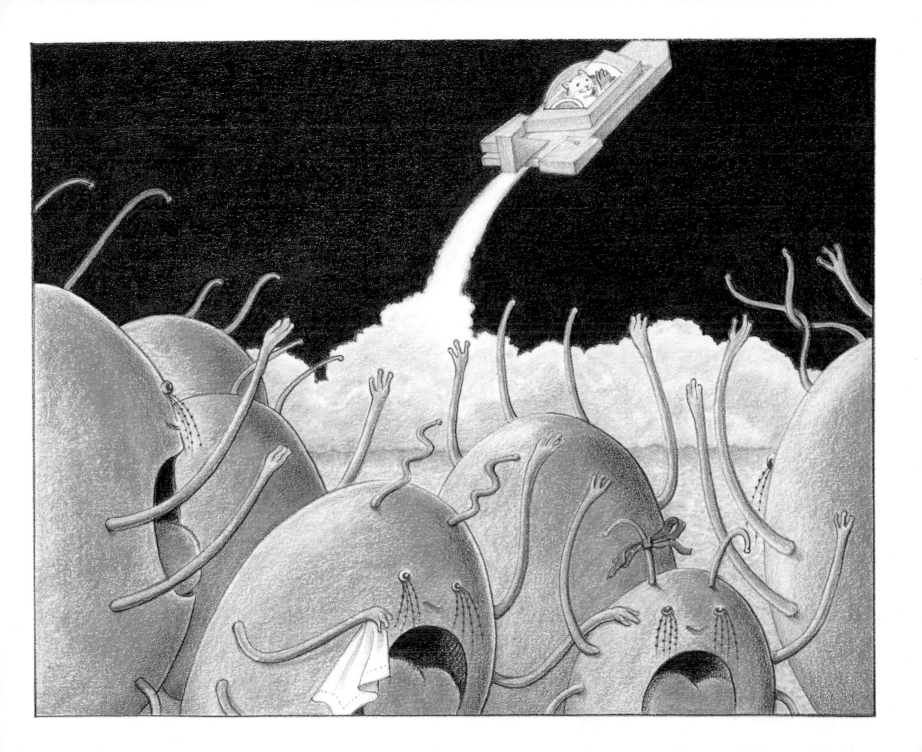

In the kitchen, Grandpa Harry was doing the dishes. "I've lost SPACESHIP NUMBER FOUR," Molly told him. Grandpa stared into the sinkful of bubbly water. "Sorry," he said. "Nothing here."

The only other place Molly could think of was the front hall, but all she found there were hats and boots and coats and umbrellas. "It must really be lost!" she cried.

Then, just as Molly was thinking she might have to start work on SPACESHIP NUMBER FIVE, she heard a stupendous whoosh, a tremendous thump, and a loud scratching at the front door. It sounded like Mordecai, asking to be let in. Molly ran to the door and opened it.

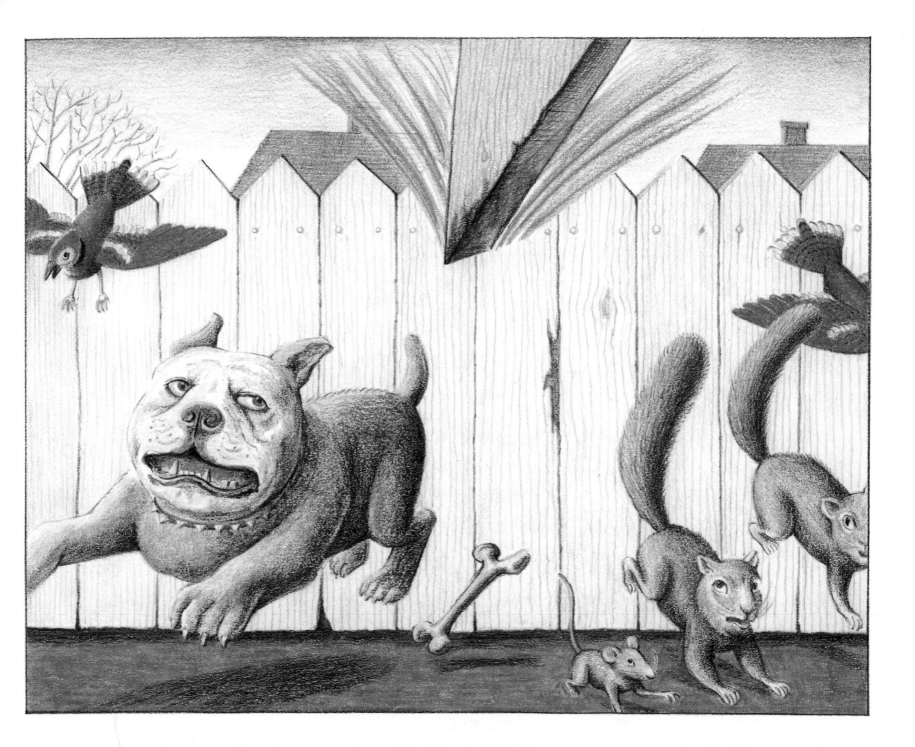

There, slightly charred but still very serviceable, was SPACESHIP NUMBER FOUR!

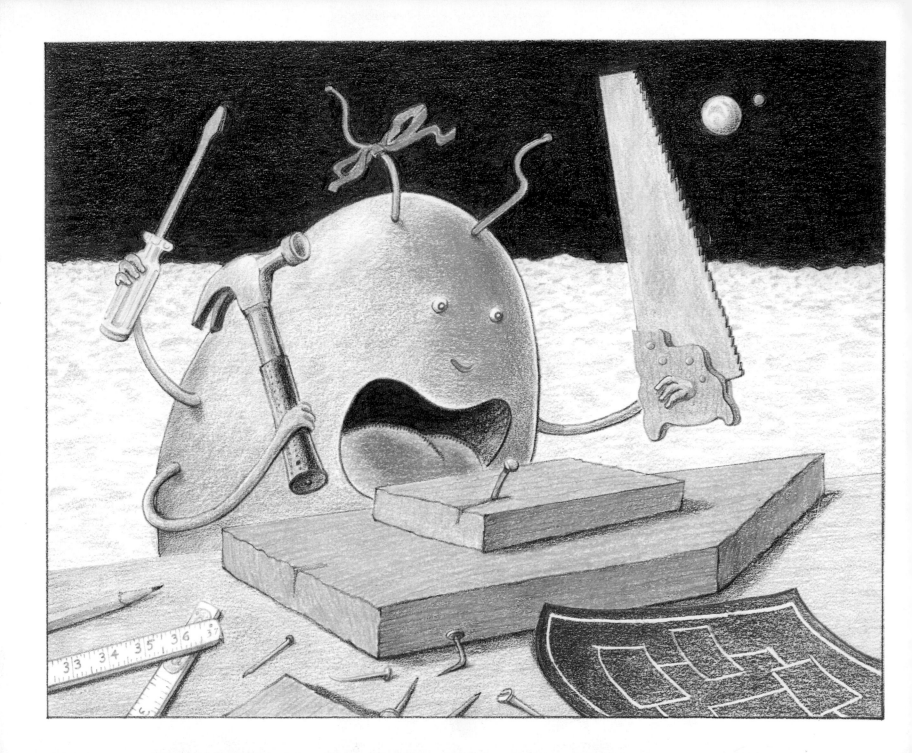